Rockets

SILLY SAUSAGE

Sausage and the Little Visitor

Michaela Morgan
& Dee Shulman

A & C Black • London

For Lulu, the real little Sausage

Rockets series:

CROOK CATCHERS - Karen Wallace & Judy Brown

MOTLEY'S CREW - Margaret Ryan & Margaret Chamberlain

MR CROC - Frank Rodgers

MRS MAGIC - Wendy Smith

MY FUNNY FAMILY - Colin West

ROVER - Chris Powling & Scoular Anderson

SILLY SAUSAGE - Michaela Morgan & Dee Shulman

WIZARD'S BOY - Scoular Anderson

First paperback edition 2001
First published 2001 in hardback by
A & C Black (Publishers) Ltd
35 Bedford Row, London WC1R 4JH

ISBN 0-7136-5472-4

A CIP catalogue record for this book is available
from the British Library.

Printed and bound by G. Z. Printek, Bilbao, Spain.

Chapter One

Sausage is a long, low dog. He's as long and as plump as a sausage. That's why he's called... Sausage.

Today he's a very, very happy Sausage.

Today Elly and Gran have been playing with Sausage.

All day long they played with him.
They gave him lots of attention.
They tickled his fat little tummy.

Tickle

Tee Hee

They stroked his long floppy ears.

And they played *Fetch!* and *Catch!*

5

At first Sausage wasn't very good at Fetch and Catch.

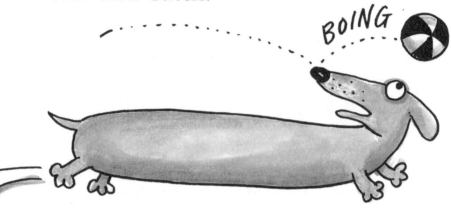

But he's getting better...

...and better.

He still makes a few mistakes.

Wrong ball, Sausage!

oops!

But Gran and Elly call him...

7

Fitz and Spatz are very snooty cats.
They call him...

Chapter Two

Even though the cats laughed at him,
Sausage knew that Elly and Gran and
Jack loved him...

...and so Sausage was a happy little Sausage until the day that...

...Jack came home from school with another pet!

Elly and Gran seemed to agree.

'But I'm the one who's little and sweet and fat and funny,' thought Sausage.

But nobody was looking at him.

Nobody was looking at the cats either.

Chapter Three

After Hammy arrived,
everything changed.

Daytimes weren't the same.
Playtimes weren't the same.

And night-times were awful!

Hammy never slept through the night.

Sausage did all his best tricks.

He rolled over.

He begged.

He balanced a sausage on his nose.

But nobody seemed to care.

Sausage was fed up.

So were the cats.

Go Hammy!

Come on Hammy!

21

Chapter Four

'I think it's time to sort that little rodent out,' said Fitz.

'I think so too,' said Spatz.

'I think it's time for
a tasty little snack,'
said Fitz.

'I think so too,'
said Spatz.

Me too!

SAUSAGE

But Sausage didn't agree with what the
cats said next.

'That little hamster would make a tasty snack,' said Fitz.

'We could have a cheese and hamster sandwich,' said Spatz.

'Or hamster and chips.'

'Or a hamsterburger!'

'We'll wait till nobody's looking, then...
...we'll pounce.'

Chapter Five

'I've got to warn Hammy,'
thought Sausage.

So off he went.

But when he got to Hammy's cage
what did he find?

'He's escaped! He's out of his cage!'
cried Sausage.

'All the better for us,' purred the cats,
and they sharpened their killer claws.

'I've got to find Hammy.
I've got to find Hammy,' thought Sausage.

And he set off to follow the trail.

At first it was easy.

But after a while Sausage had to use his
special dog skills.

sniff
sniff

He sniffed out the trail and followed it.
But the cats followed him.

Sneakily...

...the cats crept after him.

A hunting we will go,
A hunting we will go,
We'll find a snack and then
snap snap,
We'll never let it go!

Sausage went from room...

...to room...

...to room...

...up and up until
he was in the loft.

Fitz and Spatz were not far behind.

In the loft it was very dark. It was very
quiet and it was very dusty.

Achoo!

sniff

sniff

sniff

But Sausage followed the trail.

He had to tiptoe through some strange shapes.

He had to teeter over some high beams.

It was tricky.

It was very, very tricky.

But bravely, Sausage carried on until
he finally found Hammy.

The little hamster
was curled up and
snoozing after his
long journey.

'It's all right now,'
cried Sausage.

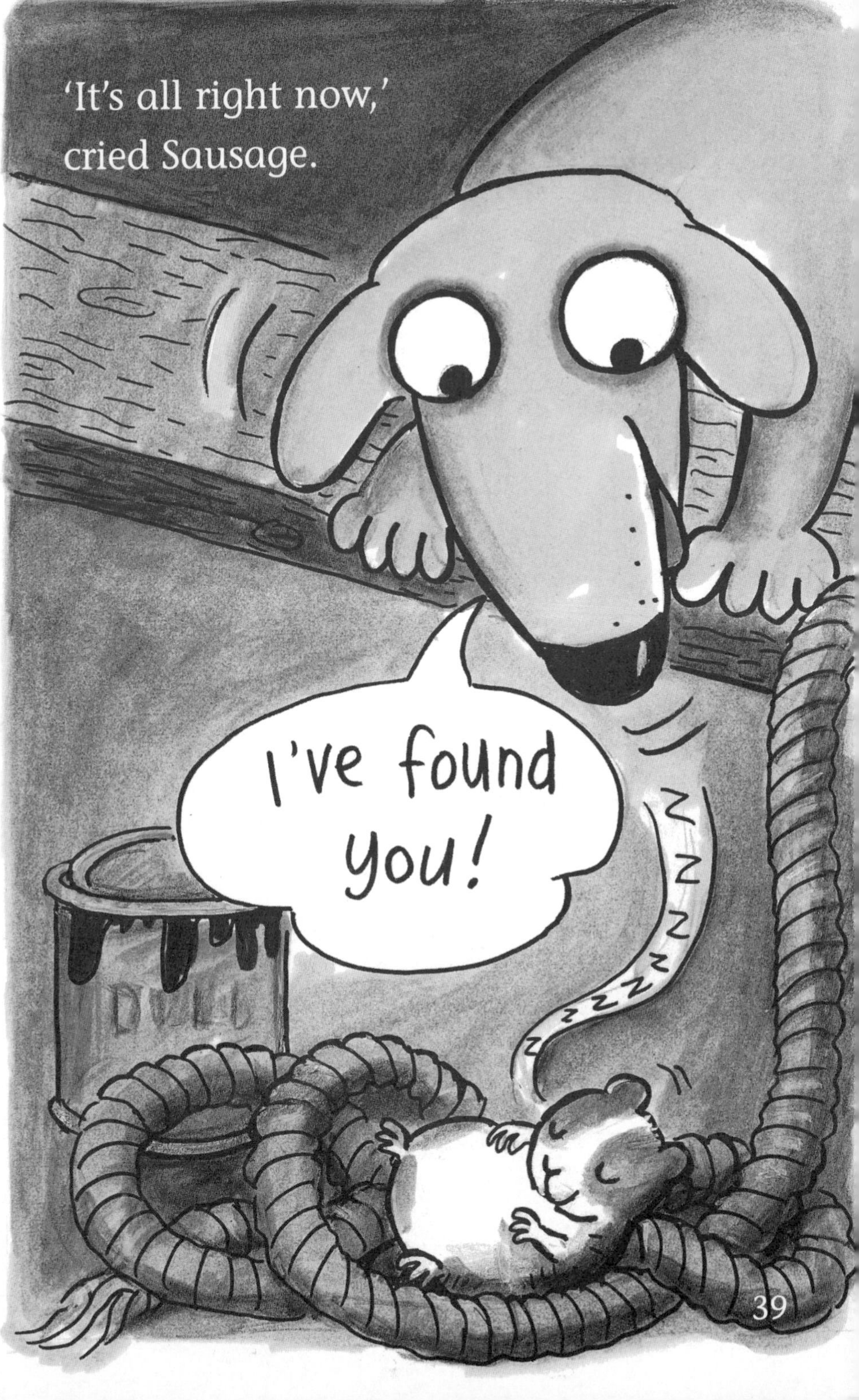

Unfortunately, Fitz and Spatz the
hunting cats spotted him at the
same time.

The hamster woke from his
dreams of nests and nuts.

'I dreamt of nuts!'
he said.

Then he saw the cats. 'Oh nuts!' he said.

The cats pounced...

...and just at that moment...

...Sausage teetered and toppled...

...and fell.

He turned twice in the air, did a...

...little back flip and...

...landed on something soft.

It was the two snooty cats.

Gran saw what had happened.

'Well done Sausage!' she said.
'You've saved the day...
...and the hamster!'

And so Sausage and Hammy became best of friends. And Sausage and Hammy got lots and lots of attention.

And both the cats got told off.